CHRISTMAS, HERE I COME!

To Don Bluth, Gary Goldman, and John Pomeroy—DJS

For Chloe and Emma—LS

GROSSET & DUNLAP
An Imprint of Penguin Random House LLC, New York

Text copyright © 2021 by David Steinberg. Illustrations copyright © 2021 by Laurie Stansfield.
All rights reserved. Published by Grosset & Dunlap, an imprint of Penguin Random House LLC, New York.
GROSSET & DUNLAP is a registered trademark of Penguin Random House LLC.
Manufactured in China.

Visit us online at www.penguinrandomhouse.com.

Library of Congress Cataloging-in-Publication Data is available upon request.

ISBN 9780593094242   10 9 8 7 6 5 4 3 2 1 HH

CHRISTMAS, HERE I COME!

BY D. J. STEINBERG

ILLUSTRATED BY LAURIE STANSFIELD

GROSSET & DUNLAP

WHEN CHRISTMAS COMES TO TOWN

The wind's a little blowier,
the sky's a little snowier,
our street's a little glowier
when Christmas comes to town.

My step's a little springier,
the songs are so much singier,
bells ring a little jinglier
when Christmas comes to town.

4

My cocoa cup is steamier,
our house is always gleamier,
and all the world seems dreamier
when Christmas comes to town!

ALL THE TRIMMINGS

There's a box in the basement, all bundled and tied,
we take out once a year . . . Want to see what's inside?
Ornaments, baubles,
a snowman that wobbles,
silvery tinsel, cottony snow,
pine cones and berries and faux mistletoe.
Out they all come! I can't wait to see
how they all look on this year's Christmas tree.

GINGERBREAD SKYSCRAPER

It started off as a gingerbread house
just like it showed on the paper,
but then we kept going until we had made . . .

a gingerbread skyscraper!

A LETTER FOR SANTA

Dear Santa Claus,

For Christmas this year, I would like

- peace on earth
- an end to war
- no more hunger anymore
- no more bad things
- no more sad things
- only happy things in store

and if that's too much, I'd settle for

- *Mega-Zombie-Racers 4!*

Many thanks,

Bobby

PICKING A TREE

For us all to agree on *one* perfect tree,
it may take the whole day, who can tell?

But we don't really care how much time we spend there 'cause we love that fresh Christmas tree smell!

SANTA CLAUS AROUND THE WORLD

If you meet a guy in Paris
with a beard and bright red pants,
that's "Père Noël," *not* Santa Claus,
'cause that's his name in France.

But when he goes to Russia,
Santa's red snowsuit gets tossed,
'cause there he likes to dress in blue
and go by "Father Frost."

He's "Sinterklaas" in Holland,
"Santa-san" in Japanese,
and if you're in Hawaii,
"Kanakaloka" if you please.

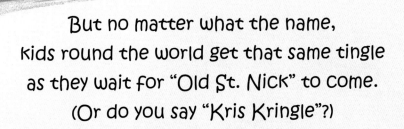

But no matter what the name,
kids round the world get that same tingle
as they wait for "Old St. Nick" to come.
(Or do you say "Kris Kringle"?)

TEN THINGS TO DO ON WINTER BREAK

School is out the whole week through!
So many, many things to do—

1. Sleep late.

2. Watch TV.

3. Stay in pj's till a quarter to three.

4. Have hot chocolate in my big red cup.

5. Put my coat on and bundle up.

6. Make snow angels.

7. Climb a tree.

8. Go night sledding with my family.

9. Come home tired from a wacky day of fun.

10. Start again at number one!

ELF SCHOOL

I heard there's a school at the North Pole
where elves learn how to make toys.
I think that I'm going to apply there
and live with those elf girls and boys!
I tell Mom and Dad my decision,
and they say, "Okay, well, have fun."
But I change my mind when they mention
the weather is forty below in the sun!

A FUNNY THING ABOUT CHRISTMAS

All children with white Christmases
want someplace warm to go,
while children living in the sun
are dreaming of the snow!

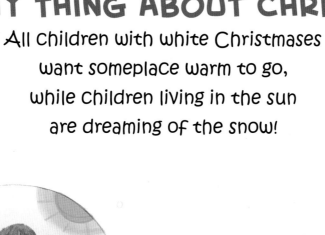

PEACE ON EARTH

Mr. Jones hung up some lights
to decorate the festive nights.
Then Mr. Smith, what did he do?
He hung his own lights up, times two!
So Mr. Jones put up some more.
Then Mr. Smith did, too, times four!

So many Christmas lights that . . . *SPARK!*
The circuits blew and all went dark.
And there they sat that Christmas night
without a single shred of light.
They lit one flame to warm their bones,
and that's when Misters Smith and Jones
shook hands at last, their battle through.
"Peace on earth," said Jones.
Said Smith, "Times two."

MY CHRISTMAS SWEATER

My sweater's just ridiculous
with pictures of Saint Nicholas.
The right sleeve sports a massive hole.
It smells like green bean casserole.
It's so big, it's preposterous.
It might fit a rhinoceros.
But my sweater's still the snuggliest—
who cares if it's the ugliest?!

ANOTHER LETTER FOR SANTA

Dear Santa Claus,

Why does the whole world leave cookies
for your midnight snack when you visit?
That must be a billion calories,
which can't be too healthy, now is it?

That's why I decided this Christmas
to put broccoli instead on your shelf,
and because we don't like to waste food at our house,
guess I'll just eat your cookies myself.

your concerned
friend,

Bobby

MADE BY ME

I gave Mom a box made of Popsicle sticks
that wobbles a bit on the bottom.
My dad got a pen holder made from a can—
I think all the dads at school got 'em.
I don't really have any money
to buy fancy gifts from the mall,
but Mom and Dad tell me the presents I make
are the very best presents of all!

THE FIREPLACE WIZARD

My mom's the fireplace wizard. She takes one little match.
She lights a tiny wisp of flame and waits for it to catch.
Soon golden flickers fill the room. She makes the flames dance higher.
Our family all gathers to admire Mom's magic fire!

THE WONDERS OF FRUITCAKE

Fruitcake is good for many things—
so fruity, dense, and thick.
It makes an excellent doorstop.
It makes for a very fine brick.
It's useful as a stepping stool.
As a paperweight, you can't beat it.
But pretty, pretty, pretty *pleeeeeeeeease*—
just don't make me *eat it!*

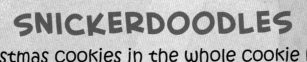

SNICKERDOODLES

The king of Christmas cookies in the whole cookie kit and caboodle
is the cinnamon-sweet, crisp and crumbly treat—
that tasty snickerdoodle.
Start with one and you're going to want oodles.
You can keep your biscotti and strudels.
I'd give twelve Christmas pies and a Truffle Surprise
for a plate of fresh-baked snickerdoodles!

HOLIDAY BOOK DRIVE

I pick out a book at the bookstore,
even though I've already read it.
That book was so great,
it's the one I'll donate
so some other kid's sure to get it!

C-C-COLD CHRISTMAS CAROLERS

Why do Christmas carolers
stick so close together?
If not, they'd turn into icicles,
out in that *c-c-cold* Christmas weather!

FINALLY!

At the first ray of Christmas morning,
I bound out of bed to see.
"He was here!" I wake the whole family.
"There are presents under the tree!"

THE BEST MESS EVER

The halls are decked with wrapping paper.
There are boxes all over the place.
Did you guess from this mess we just opened our gifts?
Or was it the smile on my face?

TIME TO EAT!

The house smells like mashed potatoes
and Grandma's mint-roasted lamb,
with notes of corn bread and pudding
and a hint of honey-glazed ham.

When at last we sit down to the table,
there is so much to eat, I can't wait!
But *uh-oh!* There's a serious problem.
There is not enough room on my plate!

ONE LAST LETTER FOR SANTA

Dear Santa Claus,

You worked so hard this Christmas
while the rest of us stayed home to play,
which doesn't seem too fair to me—
we should give you a holiday!
Maybe a week in Tahiti
with your wife and those elves and reindeer?
Then once you're refreshed, you can get back to work,
'cause I'm starting my list for next year!

Happy New Year,
Bobby